BITTERSWEET

BITTERSWEET

TAMI FIORE

Tami Fiore

First published in 2018

ISBN: 978-1-976-99047-2
Coverdesign: Tami Fiore

To mum and dad who raised me
with the love of an entire universe.
And to my favorite sister.
So she won't get jealous.

Contents

BITTERSWEET

Your behavior feels like drinking a glass of roses
Their thorns harm my heart
While I'm tasting each blossoms' flavor
What a bitter sweet drink

BITTER

heart Affairs

bittersweet

I was quiet
But not blind
My tears had colors
One for each
It were a lot
During our whole time together
The hardest question
I asked myself
Was if I should let it die or
If I should even try harder

Untruthful

Sometimes people act

As if they were victims

But deep down inside

They know they aren't

Let them be the ones

They want to be

Their fear is caused by jealousy

Just stay away

From their toxic souls

bittersweet

This little girl sitting there

Her eyes full of fear

Chained in her own thoughts

I want to rescue her

Unchain her soul

Dry her tears

After staring at her for a while

I noticed

Her was me

- *We just can free ourselves*

Broken promises
You only were fantasy to me
Your love was like a ghost
I thought I saw
You're not guilty of
My disappointment
I embarrassed myself
By letting you
Kill my feelings
Slowly

Self-destruction

You bury your fears in anger

Thinking others abused your care

But you did not notice

The person who needed your care the most

Was You

You already suffered from frostbite
In your heart
When I left
Because you already had
Turned cold
Long time ago

bittersweet

You unwrapped me
Like a gift on a birthday
Until I stripped to the buff
But all you wanted
Was to control me
'Cause you did not
Believe in true love
So you took off
My emotions
And used them
For your pleasure
Afterwards you accused me
Of betrayal

bittersweet

You are like a cigarette
Everybody seems to need you
But the only thing you really do
Is poison them

bittersweet

How could I blame you
For not loving me
Since you never learned to love
Yourself at all

I was afraid
To fall in love
With you
Because I was afraid
To be the only one
Who falls

bittersweet

You gave me access to your body
But never to your heart

I do not wonder
Why you are alone
I just wonder why
I needed so much time
To get it

bittersweet

I wanted you
More than
Everything
But you
Wanted everything
More than
Me

The strongest move
I could ever make
Was away from you

bittersweet

You hate me because I left
But although you continue playing
On all women in the world
You'll still end up being alone
- *cheater*

bittersweet

You cannot expect your flowers to grow
When you do not water them
How do you think our love will grow
When you also missed to water
The seeds of our hearts

The love I gave to you

Hurt me

The love you did not give to yourself

Hurt us both

- *mutual suicide*

The walls were shaking

When your voice burst against 'em

Disturbing the neighbors

Like loud music

While you were shouting at me

I did not hear anything but fear

- *insecurities*

Unfair

If I would've been

Honest to myself

I would've told you earlier

That I used you

To get over him

I wrote

But not for you

The sun shone

But not for us

- *end of a relationship*

bittersweet

I did not
Lose your
Love
'Cause it
Was Never
Mine

Why do you feed me with words

I cannot eat

You give me a glass of lies

I cannot drink

You bake cakes of love

And poison them with hate

Don't let unsaid words suffocate you

She felt mistreated
And gave the blossom of guilt to me
She was a rose but didn't know
Harmed others with her thorns
To protect herself

bittersweet

It's so nice how my heart lies to myself
For loving people who don't deserve it
For letting them into my mind again and again
Cutting off all my organs of love
And give 'em back when used

You lied

To protect yourself

I believed

To protect myself

Because I knew

Catching fire
It burns inside my mind
You set my heart on fire
Incinerating my body
Slowly burning down my soul
Heat in my head
All you leave behind
Is just ash

The truth is like

Shapes of the clouds

People see

Only what they want to see

- *rumors*

bittersweet

Snowflakes kissing my nose
Falling from the dark night sky
Like shooting stars
And all I miss
Is you
But all I smell
Is loneliness

Chasing orgasms
As if they were the only feeling
That could let vanish all the pain
For single moment

Sometimes I fear
The moon could fall
And the sun will never
Rise again
- *insecure future*

Your fingers caress my thigh

As if you could feel

The touches I need

Sitting here between all the strangers

Waiting for our train to arrive

Feeling lost in this foreign country

- *soothing*

bittersweet

It was
As if you
Wrote your messages
With sips of whiskey
'Cause I never understood
Your inner firestorms

Your body looks like a juicy cherry
But your heart is poisonous like its stone

bittersweet

I do not understand why
The less I love you
The more you try to keep me
But when I love you the most
The less you want me

You covered me in words

Like snow covers everything in beauty

But when I thought

I would shine

Sun melted all and uncovered

The sere leaves

- *liar*

We were sleeping in one bed

Sharing blankets

Dreams and future plans

I gave you wings to fly

When you tore me down

I lifted you up

And you went on

Destroying me

- *mental abuse*

bittersweet

Your absence felt like a knife in my back

Every day I missed you terribly

Until one day I realized

I did not

Miss you

In fact I only

Missed my old self

I did not know what
I served you for
But all I saw was
I could help you
Being the punching bag
You could throw your sorrows at
- *false friends*

No new beginning

I wanted

To love you

More than

I loved anybody else before

Love changes

And before

I could love you

Entirely

I needed to stop

Loving him

But maybe

I never did

bittersweet

Every night
Feels like a step towards the end of our days
I hate to be the reason of somebody's tears
But if you want butterflies in your stomach
You have to eat cocoons

They looked at each other like prisoners
Not knowing that they were
Prisoners of their thoughts
Prisoners of their fears
Prisoners of themselves

bittersweet

Whenever you play with words
Be careful
Sometimes tears fall off the sky
Because your cloudy words
Cause inner storms
And not sunrays remain
But scars

Sweet honey running down my cheeks

Finding its way to my lips

A jar full of tears - tasting like salt instead

Fire in my heart
Enthusiasm in my soul
Tremor in my mind

bittersweet

Your fears fit into my pocket
And I safely carry them around
With me
All the time
Just to be sure
That you're hurting us
Both

bittersweet

My body is canvas
My scars are art

My smile is a painting
My thoughts are the colors

My skin is paper
My wrinkles are words

My tears are the rubber
But my view remains blurred

- solid storyteller

People tend to suck everything off my soul
Then leave

bittersweet

There are no words for the heat in my chest
There is no description for the fire in my body
My face is burning, my cheeks are red
But my heart is cold
I keep my fears locked up

I know you, he told her
He didn't
I am there for you, he told her
He wasn't
I will change, he told her
He didn't
I am faithful, he told her
He wasn't

I love you, he told her
But she didn't
Believe
Anymore

Cruelty to a soul
While she sacrificed herself
For his mental health
He made her suffer
And feel worthless
Trapped her in a cage of emotional addiction
She barely could not escape from

You cannot turn me on
Just by pushing a button
- *egoism*

bittersweet

Don't even think
Of touching
My soul
With your dirty hands

Your side of the bed

Went cold

Whilst you still

Were lying there

So I had to leave

Before I

Would've started

To suffer

From trembling

bittersweet

Your memory burns

Inside my chest

You keep on destroying

My hope

That one day you'll

Leave

My heart

Forever

I wanted to heal you
But all I needed
Was to heal myself

bittersweet

I care for the scars
You left on my soul
I moisturize them
I caress them
I help them to disappear
But they still hurt at times
They still are dry and cracky
Sometimes
They are signs of
Your weakness
But also of my
Strength

You cannot pick up a sunflower silently
But a daisy
Because everybody notices sunflowers
Whilst daisies are invisible

bittersweet

Her thoughts were like waves
Bursting against the rocks
Her feelings were like the ocean
Short-tempered and intense
He wanted to dance with her heart
But they didn't have the same rhythm
He saw the world through a mask
He was blinkered
He didn't see her
Although she was there all the time

bittersweet

Voices flushing through my head
Confusing noises
Some of them are lies
Some of them are truth
But where's yours?
- *searching for inner peace*

bittersweet

My mind
Is captured in
A cage full of self-doubts
And you
Keep feeding it

I left myself

To open

The doors

To your universe

But all you saw

Was a stranger

Standing in front of

Your door

And you did not

Even think of

Letting me in

- *self-loss*

bittersweet

I am a rock and

You are the sea

Your waves cover me

But I always appear again

Even stronger

I wanted to protect you

From your fears

But all you saw is

How I was doing

Good

Whilst you were continuing

To struggle

You could not resist

The temptation

But tear me

Down

- *weakness*

bittersweet

You wanted
To sell me your
Truth
But I instead
Chose to keep
My own reality

You only needed
To get rid
Of your emotional trash
By taking my
Good faith for granted

In the same moment
You decided to
Show me
Your weakest point
'Cause you left
Yourself
And gave the guilt
To me

At the beginning
Our love was
Like diving
I felt
Weightless
But suddenly
You took off
All the oxygen
And I suffocated
Slowly

My dear
A man who's searching
For mistakes in your past
Does not deserve
Anything of your future

You hit me

Like a car on the street

I didn't look for

You destroyed me

By just passing by

And taking all life

With you

- fallen out of love

My blood ran cold

Whilst I realized

The only thing

You wanted

Was my pain

And you admitted

That this would be

The only option

To stop yours

The punches you

Harmed my body with

Weren't the things

That really hurt

It was the message

You sent

By violating

The only one

Who really loved you

Unconditionally

bittersweet

You don't grieve
For me
You grieve
For the part of yourself
You lost
When I left
- *remembrance*

I never cursed you

Although you hurt me

'Cause all you needed

Was love

You got

But did not

Recognize

bittersweet

The day I will be totally free
Will be the day you'll leave
My mind
Forever

You're like a mountain in a jar
You need so much space
To grow
But all you think you deserve
Is a little shed without windows

She still flinches

While looking into a mirror

'Cause she always sees the shadows

Of the pain

You caused

Although you aren't there

Anymore

bittersweet

Your smile always makes me wonder

If you sometimes cry

As hard as you smile

Every time I see you

And if you're hiding something

Behind your shiny teeth

That has nothing to do with

Sunshine

- *actor*

Yes, I still water my plants
Although they're about to die
'Cause one day
They will bloom again
And all they need now
Is my care
In their darkest moments
And so you do, too

I break easily
There's nothing I can do
Against it
'Cause when I love
I do it with every
Piece
Of me
Unconditionally

It's not

That I

Don't love

You

But I

Love

Myself

More

SWEET

a Sea full of lovers

bittersweet

When your lips meet mine
Two worlds burst against each other
The intimacy of two oceans kissing the offshore
Warm and cold water drops mixing up
Arising as a new sea of love

No matter how hard your inner storms might be
I will always be there to tame 'em
- *reminder*

bittersweet

It's how you touch me
The way you grab my knee
Whilst reading unimportant messages
On your phone
Not concentrating on the rush
And I can feel all the safety in the world

Note to my future husband
You are a hell of a drug to me
I adore you since day one
Universe caused we met each other
While the sun tried to burn my eyes
My heart was set on fire

I'll never get tired of watching sunsets
As well as I'll never get tired of loving you

Wine is why hearts are red

It's just how you hold your glass of wine

Every drop that kisses your lips

The way it reddens your tongue

Each sip running down your throat like caresses

Directly to your heart

Sometimes I wonder how life

Has been before you

bittersweet

I don't just wanna tell you that I love you
I just wanna make you feel it

Feel yourself

Be yourself

Enjoy yourself

Just

Be

You

That's enough

You replied: "...because you are everything to me."

bittersweet

If you'd be seasons
You'd be the first flower in spring
You'd be the first sunray in summer
You'd be the first colored leaf in autumn
You'd be the first snowflake in winter

If you'd be weather
You'd be the storm that's in my heart
You'd be the sun that burns my skin
You'd be the rain that calms my soul
You'd be the thunderbolt that lightens the sky
You'd be the snow that covers everything in beauty

bittersweet

How can somebody's eyes contain

So much beautiful

Sparkling brown

Like golden toffee

I can see a whole world in your eyes

If you just could see it

On your own

Happiness comes in laughter

In flowers

In sunrays

In caresses

In lovers

bittersweet

You loved me
When I was not
Able to love myself

bittersweet

You're a honeycomb
I'm standing below you
Hoping that parts of your sweetness
Will drop down on me
Kissing my nose
Running down to my lips
So that I can taste your sugar

Free like a bird

Despite you will always return to

Your safe known home

- *unchained*

You could hurt me bad
You'd despite have my back
I'd give you my heart
As long as you'd promise me
Your happiness
- *sisters*

When you lost my two little brothers
You decided to give the love
You saved for them
To me and her
On top you sacrificed yourself
For our wellbeing
Always and forever
- *affection of a mother*

It's a dark moment
And I realize
Your love
Is what I needed
The most
- *Dad*

bittersweet

The sea appeared
And so did your smile
Your eyes began to sparkle
And my soul found peace

I need your love

Until I can love myself again

'Cause my heart is like a grenade

If you let it go

It will explode

bittersweet

Love me as strong as your hugs promise

bittersweet

You twist my golden curls
Around your fingers
Feeling the sunrays
That got tangled in it
You kiss my nose
And I give back the stars
To your moon
So we can shine together
- *hearts of gold*

bittersweet

You sip on your whiskey
And I still hold my glass of water
You are the wave
And I am the ocean
You are always save
With me

A faces' beauty is chosen
By love

Leave your negative thoughts

Out of your mind

Like you

Leave your dirty boots

Outside

Before entering

Your home

Your hands feel
Like patches on my wounds

For women like me
Love is black or white
I don't know grey
And never did

Your love kisses me
With its soft lips
Your love whispers
It'll save me
From all demons
Inside me
- *lifesaver*

bittersweet

I feel insecure
And you hold me
Tight
You feel insecure
And I love you even
More

bittersweet

Maybe I've been hurt
One time too much
But I won't ever
Give up on love

bittersweet

Wrap your body around mine

Cover me with yours

Like my tattoos do

And never leave me

'Cause they neither do

bittersweet

I don't regret giving all of me
To people who never seem to appreciate it
Because it's them who need all of me
'Cause they are still searching for all
Of themselves in others

I was untouchable until then
But your knee touched mine
As if it already knew
That we belonged together

There is no disinfection
For my dirty mind

bittersweet

You touch me deep under my skin
With your big soft hands
You grab my heart
And I can feel it purely every time

I won't get sober anymore
'Cause I'm too drunk of love
- *incurable*

bittersweet

Lick my honey
Bury your fears to
Drown in my water
Taste the sweetness
Of my pleasure
While I am shaking

You're like a pumpkin

Fruit to one

Fear to the other

- *love*

In golden leaves I showered
Whilst you undressed your trees
I washed my hair with autumn breeze
And filled my lungs with oxygen
- *forest*

You were like a daisy
I saw you when no one did
I watered you with love
Then you turned into a monster
A lily with thousands of buds
Nothing left to love
The daisy's blossoms died
But you left your roots in my mind
I hope you'll have the chance to flower again
Stronger
Healthier
Better
Kinder

You cannot heal my wounds

But you can lick 'em to speed up the healing

You cannot take off my fears

But you can hug me to make 'em disappear faster

You cannot fill up the sea in bottles

But you can accompany me going there

You cannot free my soul

But you can caress all the railings to soften 'em

- *a lovers' support*

bittersweet

When all leaves turn into golden honey
And the sunsets color their clouds darker
When you feel the first cold winds
Then you know we met each other again
- *autumn*

bittersweet

I'm covered in your water
I drown in you
You're an entire ocean to me
Deep
Clear
And full of emotions

bittersweet

You lead my heart through this
Foreign city
Self-reliant as you are
Not even knowing
The security I feel
Walking besides you
Dreaming with open eyes

If there just was ice cream
With the taste of your love
- *bestseller*

When I look at the mountains
I feel all their emotions in me
When I look at you
I realize you are the mountains

Your eyes tell me you're hungry
When your mouth silently opens
Your tongue caresses your lips
And all you desire is eating me

You're a stargazer
Waiting for the stars to fall
Wishing the world's in peace
- *harmony*

bittersweet

I'm not scared
To love you
With all my heart
I'm scared
You won't love me
At all

I really need your love

Like the forest needs its trees

Like the ocean needs its waves

I really live from your emotions

Washing the dirt off my soul
Never felt that easy
Just running through
The never ending autumn forest
Covered with all its colors
Letting me breathe in
Its cold light air
- *a runners' peace*

His eyes

He fucked me with his eyes

No one ever did

His smile

He loved me with his smile

No one ever did

His heart

He touched my soul with his heart

No one ever did

Drunk of love

He feels like home

If this is home

He is

his
his breath on my neck
his lips on my ear
his hands on my chest
his laughter in my eyes
his heart to my beat
his love to my soul

You pick up the most beautiful flowers
For me
Not in the way they look
But in the way they make me feel

Thinking of him
All the time

Missing him
All the time

Smiling at him
All the time

Cuddling him
All the time

Caressing him
All the time

Kissing him
All the time

Loving him
Always

Just you
Life expects you to be strong
Love expects you to be true
Society expects you to be successful
Friends expect you to be loyal
I, I only expect you to be you

Soulmate, best friend and medicine – all at once

I am a drug to you
If you use me wrong – it will kill you
If you treat me right – it will give you
The best feeling you've ever had

It isn't enough to close my eyes
And wishing you to be here
As it isn't enough to have a heart
And not using it

I've fallen for you
Like the October leaves
Trees preparing for winter
Like my body's preparing for love

If love is your drug

I am the dealer

You need to get addicted

As I live from the earnings

You put your arm

Around my shoulders

Like the sun puts her rays down

Onto the calm sea

bittersweet

I look up to the stars
Into the beautiful night sky
And before I realized
What I really saw
You blinked slightly

Nobody loves too much

Love is unlimited and free to everyone

People often love too little

That's the problem

Who told you

The lie

That you are

Easy

To forget

Nothing
Is ever
Forever

You know where to touch me
You grab my heart
To feel my soul

Told him he's eyecandy and soulfood

He's sex, he's love, he's simplicity

He's chaos, he's sun, he's rain

He's clouds, he's storm

He's the calmness of the smooth sea

He's a thunderstorm

If he leaves there will be no more weather

In my soul

bittersweet

Your fingers caress my back
As if they were raindrops
Running down to my hips
Your hands pull my hair lightly
As if they were a gentle breeze
Covering my neck
And you whisper into my ear
That even Zeus loves my thunderstorms
So much that he wants
To take the raindrops with him
And let the sun
Dry all the tears I've ever cried

Feel alive

Don't care about what others say

Separate yourself from toxic people

Save your soul

And then I asked

You to

Please drive

Carefully

'Cause you normally

Drive me

Crazy

He smiled at her
And she immediately was trapped
In his soul

Sometimes I wonder
How universe deals with
People like you
As you are my universe
There can't be another

I put my hands
Onto your chest
To feel
How fast your heart beats
When I am close
To you

bittersweet

I want the sky
To know you
Because galaxies
Aren't built
Without stars

Dear lovely reader,

thank you for choosing my book.
For appreciating my art, my words.
I wrote this book with all my heart.
And to clean my soul from all the demons inside of it.
To find my true self and to let you know that you
aren't the only one who suffers from something.
And I promise, if you're not already doing so, one day
you will love again, even deeper.

xoxo,
Tami Fiore

15189559R00102

Printed in Great Britain
by Amazon